Waterfall Bay
Lusitania Bay
Island
Hurd Point
Davis Bay
Sandell Bay
Rockhopper Bay
Precarious Point
Carrick Bay
Windsor Bay
Green Point
Caroline Point
South West Point
To Antarctica →

For Rhyll, Caryl and Joyce.
A family drawn to nature.

South with the Seabirds

JESS McGEACHIN

ALLEN&UNWIN
SYDNEY • MELBOURNE • AUCKLAND • LONDON

On a cold, windy beach a young girl sketched the seabirds.

As they soared, swooped and skimmed across the waves, she carefully drew them in her nature diary.

Her name was Mary Gillham.

Mary grew up to be a naturalist, studying strange plants and animals. It was a job that took her all around the world, from arid deserts to rocky islands.

But there were still places she wasn't yet able to visit, and one of them was Macquarie Island in the sub-Antarctic.

The year was 1959, and Antarctica was seen as a place for heroes and adventurers, not women like Mary.

Mary was not one to take no for an answer.
She wrote to politicians and people in power, explaining how important it was to study the island and the animals that lived there.

She didn't know it yet, but on the opposite side of the world three other scientists were doing the same.

At last a letter arrived.

Mary was invited to be one of the first four women to join a research expedition to Macquarie Island. They would be watched closely by the world.

They gathered at the Melbourne docks. It was a warm December day, and the icebreaking ship the *Thala Dan* gleamed in the afternoon sun.

Mary was joined by fellow scientists Isobel Bennett, Hope Macpherson and Susan Ingham.

The *Thala Dan* sailed
south for five days.

She glided across calm,
sparkling seas

and rocked from
side to side in
stormy waves.

Cups slid from their saucers and the scientists from their bunks.

Along the way they were followed by seabirds.

Giant petrels watched from above, hoping to snatch some fish. Wandering albatrosses soared on the westerly wind, some staying at sea for years at a time.

Antarctic tern

Antarctic prion

Wilson's storm petrel
Southern giant petrel
Black-browed albatross
Wandering albatross

They came at last to an island at the edge of the world.

The four scientists
boarded a boat

that became a truck

which drove them safely to shore.

Mary and the others were greeted by the smell of salt and seaweed.

Rocky cliffs rose from the ocean and the grass was bent with the wind.

Everyone got straight to work.

The marine biologists Hope and Isobel waded through spaghetti-like kelp to the coast.

They wanted to know which animals lived in the rock pools – worlds forever changing with the tide.

On the coast
they found...
Subantarctic
crabs
Sea anemones
Chitons
Sea stars
Sea urchins
Giant kelp

Mary climbed up steep cliffs to watch the seabirds.

She was curious to find out how they lived among the island's unique plants, and sad to see that introduced rabbits were damaging the landscape.

Nesting on the island, Mary saw…

Macquarie Island cormorants

Kelp gulls

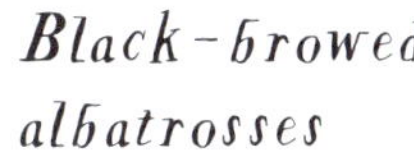

Black-browed albatrosses

Subantarctic skuas

White-headed petrels

Susan counted herds of seals.

On the beach she spotted...

They had once been hunted on the island for their fur and oil, so she wanted to know if their population was growing again.

They looked like shiny rocks lying on the black sand.

Subantarctic fur seals

Antarctic fur seals

New Zealand fur seals

Everyone watched the penguins.

It was summer, and hundreds of thousands had come to the island in their best suits to find the perfect partner.

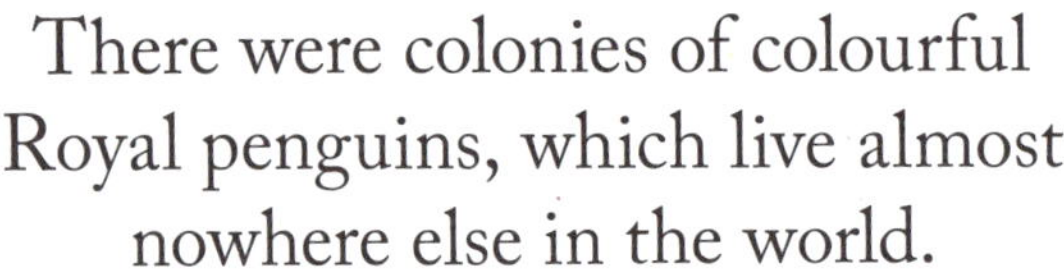

There were colonies of colourful Royal penguins, which live almost nowhere else in the world.

There were Kings feeding their fluffy chicks, who were chirping loudly for more.

There were Gentoos, who looked a little wobbly on land but were fast and graceful in the sea.

And there were small Southern rockhoppers with rockstar hair, jumping across the clifftops with ease.

The scientists walked back to the research station, their field notes full of wild plants and animals and their boots thick with mud.

They celebrated Christmas that night with roast chicken and plum pudding while the seals snored loudly under the stars.

All too soon it was time to go.

The scientists waved goodbye to the wild, wonderful island

and set sail for home.

Mary, Susan, Hope and Isobel arrived back to a flurry of cameras and questions.

Some newspaper reporters were more interested in what they wore than the things they'd learned, but the scientists knew the real story was about a small, precious island.

They couldn't wait to share what they had discovered.

Today, the rabbits and other introduced species have been removed and Macquarie Island is slowly starting to recover.

A team of scientists studying seabirds climb up to the plateau and look out across four bright blue lakes.

They are Lake Macpherson, Lake Ingham, Lake Gillham and Lake Bennett.
Lake Bennett
Lake Gillham

A timeline of Macquarie Island

600,000 years ago

Two tectonic plates in Earth's crust slowly squeeze together, rising above the sea and forming an island. Seeds float their way to its shores, finding a foothold and turning the rocky slopes lush and green.

1810

A sealer named Captain Frederick Hasselborough spots a lone, windy island in the middle of the Southern Ocean. He names it Macquarie Island to impress the Governor of New South Wales.

1810 –1919

News of the island spreads, and ships soon arrive to exploit its abundant animals. More than 200,000 fur seals are hunted for their skins, and later elephant seals and penguins for their blubber, which is used for oil.

1870

Rabbits, rats and other feral species are introduced to the island, devastating the native plants and animals. They erode the landscape and prey on the young seabirds.

1897–1922

The world becomes fascinated by Antarctic exploration, and Macquarie Island is visited by many famous explorers on their way south.

1911

Explorer Sir Douglas Mawson establishes the island's first scientific station, and the interest in studying its unique plants and animals grows. The station is later managed by the Australian Antarctic Division.

1919

The last oil ship leaves Macquarie Island. The metal barrels and digesters remain, rusty reminders of how much humans have taken from this small, wild place. The island is declared a wildlife sanctuary a decade later.

1959

Four scientists join a research trip to Macquarie Island with ANARE (Australian National Antarctic Research Expedition). They are Mary Gillham, Susan Ingham, Hope Macpherson and Isobel Bennett, the first women ever permitted to do so.

1997

The island is added to the World Heritage List.

2007

The Government of Australia agrees to eradicate pests on the island. In 2010, bait is dropped from helicopters, but sadly native seabirds are poisoned too. Despite this, the conservation effort shows early signs of success.

2014

Macquarie Island is declared pest free. It's the largest island in the world to achieve this level of eradication, and a reminder that we can begin to undo the damage we've done to the natural world.

2023

After much lobbying, the marine park surrounding the Macquarie Island is tripled in size. It's a fragile success, and one that comes at a time when the island is again under threat. Not from sealers or introduced species, but from human-caused climate change. Can we change our course once again?

The four scientists

'One could have lain for hours in the warm sunshine watching the gambolling mob of penguins but we had three and a half miles of rough going between us and the camp so we turned homewards to the end of the last full day's adventures on this magic sub-Antarctic isle.'

Mary Gillham's diary
Saturday, 26 December 1959

Left to right: Hope Macpherson, Mary Gillham, Susan Ingham, Isobel Bennett
Source: Museums Victoria

Hope Macpherson

Hope Black (nee Macpherson) was a pioneering scientist in the field of Malacology (the study of soft-bellied animals that include snails and sea slugs).

She was the first female curator at the National Museum of Victoria, but was forced to resign because of a law preventing married women from working in the public service. Determined to keep inspiring young people, Hope went on to teach science.

Mary Gillham MBE

Mary Gillham was a British naturalist, author and conservationist. She travelled the world studying plants and seabirds, always keeping a record of what she found in her field notebooks.

Mary was passionate about sharing her love of the natural world, and authored dozens of books so that everyone, not just other scientists, could understand how important these places are.

Susan Ingham

Susan Ingham was the biological secretary for the Antarctic Division, a role which saw her coordinating scientific research across Antartica and the sub-Antarctic.

Susan studied the seals and seabirds on Macquarie Island, and the data she collected is still used to understand how the animals we once hunted are slowly recovering.

Dr Isobel Bennett OAM

Isobel Bennett was one of Australia's most important marine biologists. A chance meeting led her to a job in the Zoology Department of the University of Sydney, where she led field trips around the coast of Australia and the world.

Isobel was especially interested in the inter-tidal zone (the ecosystems between high and low tide), and today her work helps us better understand places like the Great Barrier Reef.

Tips for a young naturalist

A naturalist is someone who studies the natural world. You don't need fancy tools or a certificate to start, just some curiosity and a keen eye.

Start small

You don't need to travel to the other side of the world to see how incredible nature is. Try starting in your front garden or the local park.

Research

If it's too rainy to explore, read lots of books and make sure to visit museums and libraries.

Write it down

Try drawing or writing about the things you find in a field notebook. Don't worry about making it perfect – nature is messy too.

Leave no trace

The most important part of exploring the environment is to make sure you don't damage it. Leave things as you find them, and take away only photos and field notes.

Help it heal

The natural world is under threat. It's never been more important to study and protect it, and to inspire others to do the same. Places like Macquarie Island remind us that there's always hope to be found.

The author on Macquarie Island
Image: Leila Jeffreys

This project was made possible by an Australian Antarctic Arts Fellowship.

Special thanks to Sachie Yasuda, Tiffany Brooks, Warwick Barnes, Leila Jeffreys, Flynn Jackman, Tess Chapman and the entire crew and personnel of the RSV Nuyina, V8 2023. Thanks to friends and colleagues at Museums Victoria, especially Melanie Mackenzie and Rebecca Carland, and to Julie McInnes at the Macquarie Island Conservation Foundation.

Thanks also to Alice Sutherland-Hawes, Caroline Foster, Davina Bell, Erica Wagner, Samantha Forge and Hilary Reynolds.

The Mary Gillham Archive Project (marygillhamarchiveproject.com) and Museums Victoria Collections (collections.museumsvictoria.com.au) have been invaluable resources for this project.

First published by Allen & Unwin in 2024

Allen & Unwin
Cammeraygal Country
83 Alexander Street
Crows Nest NSW 2065
Australia
Phone: (61 2) 8425 0100
Email: info@allenandunwin.com
Web: www.allenandunwin.com

Allen & Unwin acknowledges the Traditional Owners of the Country on which we live and work. We pay our respects to all Aboriginal and Torres Strait Islander Elders, past and present.

A catalogue record for this book is available from the National Library of Australia

ISBN 978 1 76106 864 5

For teaching resources, explore allenandunwin.com/learn

Illustration technique: watercolour and mixed medium

Cover and text design by Jess McGeachin
Set in 15 pt Adobe Caslon Pro by Jess McGeachin
This book was printed in September 2025 by C&C Offset Printing Co. Ltd, China.

EU Authorised Representative: Easy Access System Europe,
Mustamäe tee 50, 10621 Tallinn, Estonia, gpsr.requests@easproject.com

3 5 7 9 10 8 6 4

jessmcgeachin.com

North Head
Buckles Bay
Research station
Nuggets Point
Hasselborough Bay
Lake Bennett
Lake Macpherson
Lake Gillham
Lake Ingham
Brothers Point
Sandy Bay
Green
Gorge
Macquarie
Eagle Point
Unity Point
Bauer Bay
Mawson
Point
Cormorant
Point
Aurora
Point
Australia
New Zealand
Macquarie Island
Subantarctic
Antarctica